SUPERTATO

For my lovely dad

Thank you to Wanda Linnet for her robot picture

ALADDIN
An imprint of Simon & Schuster Children's Publishing Division
1230 Avenue of the Americas, New York, New York 10020
This Aladdin hardcover edition June 2020
Copyright © 2014 by Sue Hendra and Paul Linnet
Originally published in 2014 in Great Britain by Simon & Schuster UK Ltd.
For information about special discounts for bulk purchases, please contact
Simon & Schuster Special Sales at 1-866-506-1949 or business@simonandschuster.com.
The Simon & Schuster Speakers Bureau can bring authors to your live event.
For more information or to book an event contact the Simon & Schuster Speakers Bureau
at 1-866-248-3049 or visit our website at www.simonspeakers.com.
The illustrations for this book were rendered digitally.
The text of this book was set in Happyjamas.
Manufactured in China 0420 SCP
2 4 6 8 10 9 7 5 3 1
Library of Congress Control Number 2019940028
ISBN 978-1-4814-9037-5 (hc)
ISBN 978-1-4814-9038-2 (eBook)

SUPERTATO

Sue Hendra & Paul Linnet

ALADDIN

New York   London   Toronto   Sydney   New Delhi

Some vegetables are frozen for a very good reason. Don't believe me? Then keep reading.

It was nighttime in the supermarket, and all was quiet. But—

crash, *bang*—something had escaped from the freezer. Something small and round and green.

Something looking for trouble.
Big trouble.

"Hmmmmpfff!" cried Cucumber.

Who was doing this? And was there anyone who could help these vegetables in distress?

He used his
superspeed. . . .

He used his
superstrength. . . .

He used a washcloth
and some soapy water.

"I know who's behind this," said Supertato. "There's a pea on the loose!"

"Oh no—not a pea!" everyone gasped.

"Yes, a pea! But I'm out of the freezer now, and I'm never going back! Mwah ha ha ha ha!"

And the evil pea ran off to commit more terrible crimes.

"Time for a dip, little veggies!"

"That's enough!" shouted Supertato.

He leapt toward the pea, but the pea popped out of his hands and vanished into thin air.

Supertato set out on a supersearch.
He crept through the cakes . . .

checked the cheese . . .

and snuck up on the beans.
Then something
caught his eye.

"The game's up!" yelled Supertato.

KERPOW!

But the pea bounced out of reach and onto a cart. Supertato was just about to stop him with his superstrength

when the cart crashed—

and he was thrown down into
the icy depths of the freezer.

Was this the end for Supertato?

GASP!

Not quite.

But the pea was off his cart and lying in wait. "You're finished, Supertato!" he shrieked.

But Supertato summoned up all his strength . . .

and ran for it.

The pea nearly had him at the beans,

and closed in on him at the cheese.

The pea had him cornered at the cakes.

"So much for Supertato!" screeched the pea. "You're about to be MASHED POTATO!"

Surely, THIS was the end for Supertato?

"Not today, my friend," said Supertato.

"Gotcha!"

"Mmmppfff!" said the pea.

S Q U E

"Oh yes," said Supertato. "I set my trap, and you fell for it. Or should that be IN it?!" And he grinned a super-grin.

Supertato had saved the day.
"Take him away," he said.
And the pea was marched back
to the freezer where he belonged.

"This jelly tastes of pea!" said Broccoli. And everybody laughed and cheered.

So, remember, folks . . .

Some vegetables are frozen for
a very good reason. Maybe you'd
better go and check your freezer. Just
in case there's an escapee in your house . . .